Amadi's Snowman

A Story of Reading

Katia Novet Saint-Lot

Illustrated by Dimitrea Tokunbo

TILBURY HOUSE PUBLISHERS

Amadi crouched in the shrubs, stalking a red-headed lizard.

"Amadi!" His mother's voice boomed behind him, and the lizard scurried away. "Don't you go running about like a bush rabbit this morning. Mrs. Chikodili said she'd visit just before we leave for the market."

"Again!" Amadi was ready to bolt, himself.

"Praise the Lord! Mrs. Chikodili wants to help you with reading. For free," said his mother. "A fine boy like you—don't you want to have a good job someday, maybe in an office?"

"I'm an Igbo man of Nigeria," Amadi replied. "I'll be a trader. I don't need to read to do business."

"Business," mumbled his mother, shaking her head. "What do you know about business?"

No sooner did she turn her back than Amadi darted into the bushes. He knew his numbers well. Why did his mother insist that he learn to read words?

Down the road, he went slowly past a few older boys washing a car. He watched as the car drove away and the boys counted their earnings. How he longed to be like them! He could clean cars as well. He could carry items for people at the market. With the money he made, he'd buy small items—matchboxes, plastic hangers, dishtowels. He'd resell or trade them. He'd be a businessman!

Just then, he spotted Mrs. Chikodili as she made her way to his home. He took off towards the market.

"Amadi, you're early today! Where is your mother?" called Mama Uche.

"Home," he replied.

"Come, take a mango," she said.

"Thank you." Amadi bit into the fruit and tore strips of the yellow peel with his teeth. He licked the sweet juice that ran down his chin.

Amadi wandered about the different stalls, breathing in the smell of ripe fruits barely down from the trees, of vegetables still fresh from the earth. He chased a couple of chickens. They ran away, cackling loudly. Women laughed as they haggled and bargained.

Amadi smiled. Why work in an office when the market was so much fun?

"Auntie, please, give me some water. My hands are sticky," he asked a merchant washing carrots in a basin.

"Amadi, my boy, good morning," she answered, and poured a little water on his hands. Amadi rubbed them together and dried them on his shorts.

A little farther the food market ended. The stalls here sold everything, from fabrics to shoes, from cooking pots to plastic buckets.

Amadi walked around. He crawled underneath the stalls and back out again. Suddenly, he noticed an older boy he knew, sitting in a space crammed with boxes. He had a book on his lap.

"Chima, what are you doing?" asked Amadi.

Chima brought a finger to his mouth, his eyes darting around. "Lower your voice. The merchant doesn't like people touching his books."

An image inside the book caught Amadi's eyes: a boy bundled up in clothes stood next to a strange animal with a nose that looked like a carrot. Everywhere around, the ground and trees sparkled, blinding white.

"What's that?" asked Amadi.

"A snowman," said Chima, not even looking up. "It's made of snow."

"Snow?" Amadi repeated.

Chima rolled his eyes. "It's frozen rainwater. It makes snowflakes, and they fall from the sky and cover everything. In some countries, they get snow during a season called winter. It's really cold." Chima turned his attention back to the book.

"Do you know how to read?" Amadi asked.

Chima frowned. "Shh! Yes. I've been learning."

"What for?"

Chima heaved a sigh. "To know more, that's what for. Did you know about snow before I told you? Now, be quiet."

Chima turned the pages, and Amadi stared at the pictures in the book, trying to make sense of what he saw. What was that big white animal-made-of-snow for? What did the boy do with him? His tongue burned with questions.

A growling voice made them jump.

"What are you doing here?"

Chima dropped the book and scampered away. Amadi picked it up.

"That Chima boy thinks my bookstall is a library," groused Mr. Ogbu, taking the book from Amadi's hands. "Give me that, unless you want to buy it!"

"What do I need a book for?" Amadi said. And he ran away, images from the picture book twirling in his mind.

On his way home, Amadi saw the older boys sitting in the shade of a flamboyant tree on the roadside. He joined them.

"Do you know about snow?" he asked.

"What's that?"

"Frozen water that falls from the sky," said Amadi.

The other boys laughed. "The only things that falls from the sky are rain and dust and too much sun," said one of them. Then they ignored him, talking of this, of that. Trade was slow—the sun was hot. Mostly, they grumbled.

Amadi watched and listened, feeling as if he was seeing them for the first time. Chima's words played in his mind. He jumped up. "I better get home before Mother leaves for the market."

But his mother was already gone. She'd be furious.

"All because of Mrs. Chikodili," he mumbled as he turned back, cutting through the bushes.

The crowd at the market had thickened, but Amadi found his mother in her usual spot, selling her cooking to people hungry for lunch.

"Here you are!" she said upon seeing him. "Some help you are to your mother. Will you at least get me some plantains so I can fry them for dinner tonight?"

"Yes, Ma," said Amadi, taking the money she handed him.

After buying the plantains, Amadi wandered toward the bookstall.
Maybe he could take another glance at the book with the snowman.
As he approached, Amadi saw Mrs. Chikodili leafing through a book.
He recognized the cover instantly and froze. Was she going to buy it?
But she couldn't! She mustn't! He wanted to run and grab it from her, but
it was too late. Mrs. Chikodili gave money to the merchant and walked away.
Amadi watched her retreating back. Slowly, his feet brought him
to the stall.

"You again?" said the merchant. "I told you I don't run a library."

Amadi shrugged. "I'm just curious. What does the boy do with the snowman in the book?"

"Ha!" said the merchant. "You should have bought it this morning, when you had the chance."

"But I don't want your book," replied Amadi. "I can't read." He stopped short, and added, "I don't need to read. I'm going to be a businessman."

The man stared at him. "And you don't think reading could help a businessman? Foolish boy!"

Amadi opened his mouth, but couldn't think of a thing to say. He backed away and brought the plantains to his mother. She was busy with customers and hardly noticed him, so he left the market.

He wandered aimlessly for a long time, kicking red dust as he went.

His mind whirled with new thoughts he hardly understood. Whenever
he looked up, the sign boards on the roadside seemed to laugh at him,
their giant letters taunting him, daring him to understand their meaning.
He'd never even noticed them before.

Late in the afternoon, Amadi reached his house, feeling lost and dejected. His mother was cooking.

"Where were you?" she asked. "I waited for you at the market."

Amadi shrugged. The sweet smell of plantains frying in palm oil drifted from the pan on the wood fire, and his stomach grumbled.

"Mrs. Chikodili just left," continued his mother. "She brought you something."

Amadi's eyes widened. "Where is it?" he asked, forgetting his hunger.

"On the bench inside," answered his mother.

Amadi ran in, his heart beating hard in his chest. It was the book with the boy and the snowman! His book!

"If you don't want it, I'll return it to her on Sunday," said his mother outside. "We can't have that nice woman wasting her time on a boy who runs away."

But Amadi wasn't listening. He turned the pages, drinking in the pictures of a white world of snow he'd never known to exist before, a world so different from what he was used to. He stared at the letters. These signs told a story, the story of the country where frozen rainwater fell from the sky.

Chima can read them, and he's an Igbo man like me, he thought. Amadi closed the book and looked at the cover. The boy seemed to smile at him, as if challenging him. Amadi smiled back. Yes, he'd learn about snow. And then he'd learn more, because when this book was finished, there'd be others. And the more he learned, the more he'd know.

"Amadi, quickly go and fetch some wood," called his mother.

Amadi went outside. "You can tell Mrs. Chikodili I'll learn how to read," he declared.